Ghost Hunter

Gettysburg Ghost Gang # 4

By
Shelley Sykes
and
Lois Szymanski

 WHITE MANE KIDS
SHIPPENSBURG, PENNSYLVANIA

This White Mane Books publication
was printed by
Beidel Printing House, Inc.
63 West Burd Street
Shippensburg, PA 17257-0708 USA

The acid-free paper used in this book meets the guidelines for permanence and durability of the Committee on Production Guidelines for Book Longevity of the Council on Library Resources.

For a complete list of available publications
please write
White Mane Books
Division of White Mane Publishing Company, Inc.
P.O. Box 708
Shippensburg, PA 17257-0708 USA

Library of Congress Cataloging-in-Publication Data

Sykes, Shelley.
    Ghost-hunter / by Shelley Sykes and Lois Szymanski.
        p. cm. -- (Gettysburg ghost gang ; #4)
    Summary: Philip, Zach, Chucky, Casey, and their ghost-friend, Corporal Jared Scott, attempt to get rid of a ghost-hunter who has come to their campground at Gettsysburg, Pennsylvania.
        ISBN 1-57249-298-8 (alk. paper)
        [1. Ghosts--Fiction. 2. Camps--Fiction. 3. Gettysburg (Pa.)--Fiction.]
    I. Szymanski, Lois. II. Title.

PZ7.S9834Gj 2003
[Fic]--dc22

                                                        2003056388

PRINTED IN THE UNITED STATES OF AMERICA

Contents

Chapter One

Scary Skelly

Philip set the tall glass of iced tea down by the visiting author. "There you go, Mr. Nesbitt."

"Thanks. It's just what I needed." Mr. Nesbitt winked a blue eye at Philip and lifted the glass for a long drink. He set it back down, exchanging it for his felt-tipped pen to finish signing the books that the store had just gotten in.

"Every one of your *GHOSTS OF GETTYSBURG* books is better than the last," Philip said. "There just doesn't seem to be an end to all the ghosts!"

"Speaking of which," Mr. Nesbitt said and shot a quick glance down the counter where Mr. Baxter, Philip's father, was writing in a ledger. "How's your friend?"

Philip started to tell him that Chucky was fine, then he realized whom he meant.

"Oh! Jared's just fine. We see him quite often, almost once a day."

Mark Nesbitt shook his head and laughed quietly. "If I hadn't seen him myself..."

"You're the only person other than us to see him. Casey, that's Chucky's sister, she knows about him now. But she won't tell anyone about him. She can't see him though, just us. I still think it must be because we were the only ones who touched his I.D. tag when we found it."

Chucky's brow furrowed as he thought about their ghost friend, Jared, and how the soldier had appeared after he'd dug up the Civil War-era military identification tag. After they got over the scare, the boys found they had a great new friend. Just like any of their other friends, Jared seemed to enjoy finding adventure on the Gettysburg campground where they all lived.

Mark Nesbitt pursed his lips and raised his blond brows. "I think you must be right."

"Would you like to see him again? I'm sure he'll come to the garden if we go out there later."

"No, that's quite all right." Mr. Nesbitt laughed. "You just tell him hello for me."

"Hey! Hi there!" Zach and Chucky came running into the camp store with towels around their middles and wet hair hanging over their foreheads.

"Hey, you two. How are you doing?"

Mr. Baxter looked up when they came bursting in. "There's no fire, guys. Walk please, and let Mr. Nesbitt do his thing. He's a busy man."

"They're fine," Mr. Nesbitt said with another wink for the newcomers who pressed against the counter.

"Don't drip on the books, Zach," Philip said.

"Did you tell him about Nightmare?" Zach whispered.

"And Boo, did you tell him about Boo?" Chucky wanted to know.

"No, I haven't had the chance," Philip said.

"Nightmare?" Mr. Nesbitt asked.

"Boo's a beagle, and he likes me," Chucky leaned over to whisper. "He's Jared's *ghost* dog!"

"Nightmare's a horse, a ghost horse. We found her owner. He was dead though," Zach said.

"Of course he's dead," Chucky hissed. "He was with Corporal Scott, in the 7th Michigan. Practically all our friends are dead, Mr. Nesbitt, except you of course."

Mark Nesbitt put his head back and laughed aloud, causing Mr. Baxter to put down his ledger and walk toward them. "Now, boys, can't you find something to do?"

"Excuse me."

Everyone turned to look at the doorway. A tall, thin man with a black goatee waved a hand in the air. "Is this where I register for a campsite?"

Mr. Baxter made a shooing motion to the boys, then gestured for the man to follow him to his ledger. The boys watched him as he passed them. Chucky's eyes widened at the sight of the man's vest. It was covered with little pockets front and back, and most of them bulged with small lumps.

"Triple cool! Wish I had one of those."

Philip thought of the way Chucky kept odds and ends in his pockets and couldn't even imagine what all he would be able to carry in a vest like that. But he didn't say that. He was struck by the man's general appearance. "He looks like Ichabod Crane."

"Only scarier looking," Zach added, looking at the man nervously.

"Fellas," Mr. Nesbitt said. "Tell me more about your latest encounters while your dad is busy."

So the boys talked quietly while the author signed his name in his books. They liked Mr. Nesbitt. Even though he was a real author, and a historian, he had come to see them when they asked him for help when Jared Scott first appeared. Besides being able to carry all those facts around in his brain, which Chucky greatly admired, the man was just plain fun for the boys to be around.

They had just finished the story about getting the ghost horse back to his ghost owner when Mr. Baxter came over again.

"Boys!" he said.

Mr. Nesbitt stood up. "Mr. Baxter, I don't mind. They're fine."

"If you say so. But here's a gentleman who would like to meet you." He reached across the counter to the stranger who had just come in, touching his shoulder. "Mark Nesbitt, meet Byron Skelly from New York. He's a fan of yours."

"Hello," Mr. Nesbitt said, extending a hand for the man to shake.

"I have the first two of your books, Mr. Nesbitt, and I can't believe my luck to find you here. I was planning to try to reach you while visiting."

"Thank you, that's nice."

"I'll buy the others here," he said, reaching for a book, "and they're even signed! You know, ghosts are a big hobby of mine. I'd love them to be my career, but you can't make a living hunting for ghosts, can you? I mean, unless you write about them, like you do."

"Are you going to be doing some ghost hunting while you're here?"

"Oh yes! That's my main reason for coming. I belong to a group at home, but they mainly investigate, and nothing else. I think there is great work to be done beyond hunting and investigating ghosts."

The boys were silent, afraid to miss any of the conversation. Mr. Baxter sighed and took the stack of books to put them in the bookracks.

The author scratched his blond head. "I have to admit that I don't see what you're getting at, but I'd be interested in hearing about it."

Byron Skelly smiled and leaned an elbow on the counter, making himself at home.

"It's just that I feel that ghosts are only here because they want to be. I think it's all right for some people to stand around with incense and such, and lecture spirits about the white light and heading into it. But if anyone knows about the white light it's the ghosts, you know? I think they *want* to stay, and they must be sent away."

Philip looked at his brother, Zach, and Chucky. They were looking at him; mouths open like the catfish they sometimes caught with Dad. This guy didn't know what he was talking about!

"Just how do you go about something like that?" Mr. Nesbitt asked.

"Ghosts are energy. Some energy repels. I try to repel them. If I'm persistent, they get irritated and go."

Zach felt a chill creep up his mind. This Mr. Skelly was scary. His eyebrows knitted as he spoke, his dark eyes intense and flashing. "But where do they go?" Zach asked.

Mr. Skelly shrugged as though answering a kid was a waste of his time. "Who cares where the ghost has gone if a family can get a good night's sleep! Ghosts don't belong here on the earth plane where they get in the way of the living."

The author put his hands on his hips. "That's interesting, but I can't say I agree with you."

"A lot of people disagree with me. But it doesn't stop me. I've got several places to check this week. I'm going to scan for signs of ghosts first, of course. Then if I get a reading, I'm going to try to get rid of them."

"You sound like a bug exterminator," Chucky said suddenly.

Byron Skelly looked down at Chucky. His smile looked forced, almost like a grimace. "Yes," he said, then he turned back to the author. "Well, it was nice meeting you, Mark."

Mr. Nesbitt nodded but didn't say anything.

"Hey, where did the books go?" Byron Skelly asked.

"Mr. Nesbitt is finished for the day. I put them away. They're over there on the racks." Philip pointed to the back wall.

Skelly nodded with half a frown. Then he turned back to Nesbitt. "Thanks. Hope to see you again."

The boys and the author watched the ghost hunter as he walked over to the books.

"Can he do that?" Zach whispered. "Can he find ghosts and make them go away?"

Mark Nesbitt leaned down to the boys and they huddled together, heads nearly touching. "I don't know, fellas. But the next time you see your friend, you'd better tell him to keep far away from that guy."

Philip saw the worry in the kind blue eyes of their author friend. Chills raced once around his neck. "Why did he have to come *here*?"

Chapter Two

Sleeping Out

"I'm glad Dad let us have a fire," Zach said while he pushed a hot roasted marshmallow on top of his piece of chocolate on a graham cracker. He tried to do it with the stick, and not get his fingers into the gooey marshmallow.

They were in the field where the jamborees took place, and Philip had a flashlight and star chart by his side. "Don't drip it on the sleeping bag," he said to Zach. Then he looked up at the sky. "It's not often we get to sleep out under the stars."

"I hope we don't get cold," Chucky said. He was sipping hot chocolate from a thermos. "This is the first time I've slept out with you guys."

Zach took a bite of his s'more. "This is the first time this summer," he said. He waved a hand in front of his mouth. "Hot!"

"You are suitably outfitted for a warm night like this," Jared said from the darkness. They turned toward his voice and watched their ghost friend enter the circle. His light blue-colored glow merged with the light. As he drew closer, the firelight flickered and danced in shadows on his dark blue uniform. "You are better suited than we were for most of our nights during the war. We had blankets and hard ground if we didn't have time to make camp," he said. He looked appraisingly at the tent behind them.

"Hey, I'm glad you could come see us," Philip welcomed him. Something about having Jared around made everything feel safe and better. Philip knew it was strange that a ghost could make him feel secure, but he'd trust his ghost friend with his life.

"Casey told me you had to see me."

"Casey did?" Chucky looked at him over the rim of his cup.

"Do you know how I always greet her with a tap or a tug?" The corporal's voice was deep, but low sounding, and the boys leaned close to hear him. "She just started talking when I ran into her near the cottage. She said you would be sleeping outside tonight, and that you had important news. She said that I should avoid a skeleton? Now what is that all about?"

The boys laughed. "She must have said Skelly," Philip said. "Sit down and we'll fill you in."

They told Corporal Scott about the strange man who had come to camp at Cavalry Ridge.

"He scares me," Zach said.

"We're afraid he could pick up on you," Philip added. "And Mr. Nesbitt, do you remember him? He said to tell you to avoid him."

"He looks like Ichabod Crane," Chucky told him when they described the man. "You know him, right?"

"Not personally," Jared said, and they all laughed.

Chucky twisted the cup back onto the thermos. "He says he can repel ghosts with energy and that you are only here because you want to be. That's not really true, is it?"

"Which part?" Jared asked. "You know yourselves that some of the fellows I know can go where they want. I've been around a bit too, especially since meeting you boys. But where would I go if I didn't want to be here?"

"Heaven?" Zach mumbled through another bite of his treat.

"Maybe." Jared scratched his chin and looked into the fire. His blue eyes were like fire themselves with the glow that was part of him. "The question isn't where I would go if I wanted to leave. The question is where I would go if this Skelly was really able to send me away."

"I don't want to think about it!" Chucky said. "It's not right. Think about Sam, the little boy. He wanted his parents, and we all helped to find them. What would have happened to him if Mr. Skelly had found him before we did?"

They were all quiet, each with their own thoughts, remembering the ghost boy they had helped reunite with his parents. Then Philip rattled the marshmallow bag. "Hand me the marshmallow fork, Zach."

"What are you making there?"

"They're called s'mores," Zach told him. "Graham crackers, chocolate bars, and toasted marshmallow sandwiches."

"Sounds like a toothache maker," Jared said with a smile.

"Guess you never had anything like that, did you, Corporal?"

"No, Chucky, I didn't. Salt pork and bread fried in the pan, or hardtack when there were slim pickings."

"What's hardtack?"

"Well, it was supposed to be like a heavy cracker or biscuit that could travel with a troop. Mainly it was like rock until you soaked it in coffee, which helped a little. Soaking it first helped kill the weevils in it, too."

"Yuck!" Zach, who had just reached for the other half of his chocolate bar, put it back down.

Jared laughed. "I'm afraid that it didn't bother many of us. It was just something that was done. And we didn't have to do without, like some of the men."

Chucky loved it when Corporal Scott talked about the war. He could read about it in books and hear about it on television, but when the corporal talked he would smile a certain way or sigh a certain way that made the facts more personal. Their friend was a better teacher than any museum or battlefield or book could ever be.

Someone down in the RV section lit a string of lanterns and they could hear the soft sounds of someone strumming a guitar.

"I think you were all brave," Chucky said, then was startled that he'd said it aloud.

"Not brave, just doing a job."

"It's a job I wouldn't want," Philip said. "I mean . . ."

"I know what you mean."

All at once, there was a high-pitched sound that came from the camping area. It was like someone tuning a radio. Philip glanced that way, wondering if they'd have trouble with someone playing a radio too loud. It came again, a squealing sound that rose and fell on the night air.

"What the heck is that?"

Someone was walking at a slow pace, and a small red light wavered here and there in front of him. It seemed like he was heading toward the field and the boys near the fire.

Another squeal and the person stopped, raised his hands, and then *FLASH*!

"What's he taking pictures of?" Philip asked.

The person made his way toward them again, and as he neared they recognized Mr. Skelly, the ghost hunter.

"Aw, man!" Zach said. "You'd better go, Jared."

Jared stood up and was starting away, but stopped when the man pointed something in their direction. It looked like a gun!

"Hey!" Philip jumped up. "What are you doing?"

"Relax," Mr. Skelly said. He laughed, and to Zach it sounded sinister. "It's a temperature gun. But it doesn't tell me much when it's near your fire."

The squeal came again. Mr. Skelly looked down at the little boxy thing in his other hand. "Now this is an electromagnetic meter, and right now it's saying that something otherworldly is near here."

"Just us. We're near here," Chucky said, wishing Jared would go. But Jared was standing, seeming very interested in this man with his meter and temperature gun.

Mr. Skelly held his hand out, and the squealing softened, then rose and died again. He took a step toward Jared. "Right there," he said. With quick moves he tucked the meter under his arm and lifted the camera he had on a strap around his neck. *FLASH!*

"I think I got something," he said.

Philip blinked his eyes rapidly. "Yeah, you got me in the eye," he said.

Mr. Skelly didn't look amused. He was looking at the back of the camera. "There it is. Take a look, boys, it's right here."

Philip looked around. Jared was gone. He joined Chucky and Zach who were standing on either side of Mr. Skelly. His camera was a digital one, and they could all see the photo he'd just taken in a little window at the back. There was Philip, mouth and eyes wide, and behind him a large round bluish circle.

"Look at the size of that orb. That's the best photo I've ever gotten."

"What's an orb?" Zach asked.

"That's an orb." Skelly held the camera out, looking slightly impatient. "Where there are orbs, there are ghosts. And this here is one strong ghost. I'm surprised you didn't feel it around you."

"I think it is smoke from the fire," Philip said. "There aren't any ghosts around here. And if there are, they belong to us, not you. Now go away and let us get on with our campfire stories."

Zach and Chucky were amazed at Philip. They'd never heard him talk to an adult like that. But their amazement quickly turned to concern as they watched the range of emotions crossing Skelly's face.

Skelly stared at Philip, his eyes narrow, his mouth tight.

"Excuse me," he said and walked away.

Philip hunkered back down onto his sleeping bag. "I think I blew it."

"I think you were awesome!" Chucky said to make him feel better. "He won't bother us again."

"I thought he was going to hit you, Philip," Zach said. He blew his bangs upward in an agitated manner.

Philip smiled at Zach, but he couldn't keep the concern from his face. "He'll be too busy bothering Jared. You know that orb was Jared."

"That meter thing was what found Jared," Zach said.

They didn't say it aloud, but they each knew if it had found him once, it could find him again. Only next time they might not be there to help.

Chapter Three

A Shadow on the Tent

The dying embers of the campfire crackled, casting shadows on the outside of the canvas. Inside, something had made Philip waken. He sat up in the dark tent. It was stuffy, but he hesitated to open the flap. What had he heard in his dream state to bring him out of sleep?

Philip reached out for his glasses, tucked inside the pocket on the side of the tent. He was slow putting them on, adjusting the stems behind his ears. He looked around the tent.

Chucky was on his side, curled up like a hedgehog, the blankets twisted around him in a tangled mess. *How can he stand blankets in this heat?* Philip wondered. Then he noticed another lump by Chucky's legs. *Boo! When had he crept into the tent?*

The ghost dog looked like a live dog, curled up with his little black nose resting on his brown spotted hind legs, but unlike a real dog, he was fuzzy around the edges, as if, when someone colored the picture of him they had gotten outside of the lines. Boo slept as peacefully as Chucky. Philip watched Chucky, whose chest rose with each breath and fell when he exhaled in a whistle that came out through his nose.

What did I hear? Maybe I imagined it.

Zach slept on his back, sprawling across the open sleeping bag, arms flung outward, mouth open wide. His blanket was at his feet. It seemed neither of them had heard anything, and even Boo's eyes were still closed in sleep.

Philip plumped the pillow behind him and sat back.

Snap! Philip flinched. He strained his ears. A rustling sound outside made him sit up straight. "Chucky! Zach!" he hissed, but neither boy moved.

Philip reached out and grabbed Zach's ankle. Zach shot up. "What!"

"Sssh! There's something out there!"

Boo raised his head and stared at Philip sleepily.

Chucky opened an eye, then both, focusing on Philip's face. "What is it?" he whispered. Beside him, Boo came to his feet stiffly. The hackles raised up on his back and a low growl rumbled in his throat.

Philip put a finger to his lips, then pointed. A shadow was growing on the side of the tent. It crawled up the side and onto the roof . . . in the shape of a man. The three boys huddled close together, hearts pounding as they watched it grow small again. Chucky's arms were wrapped tightly around Boo. No one said a word until it had disappeared.

Chucky's face went white. He looked like he might throw up. "Who do you think it is?" he stammered.

Philip shrugged, eyes wide.

"Maybe it's Dad checking up on us." Zach's voice was a shaky whisper, one that didn't sound hopeful.

"We should look," Philip said, but no one made a move to do it.

"We should," Chucky agreed. Still they stared at each other.

"Okay. I will." Philip pushed his glasses up, adjusting how they sat on his nose.

"He's probably gone now," Zach said.

"Yeah. Probably," Chucky agreed.

Philip leaned forward on his knees and slowly lifted the corner of the tent flap. When he saw nothing, he lifted it higher, scanning the field. "There," he whispered, pointing at a figure at the bottom of the field.

Boo shoved a nose out of the corner of the tent and a growl rose again, rumbling deep down inside him. Chucky pulled him back. "Boo. Ssshhh!"

Chucky and Zach huddled close, peering out at the bent shadow of a man.

"That's not your dad," Chucky said.

The figure turned, his hand outstretched, holding something out.

"Skelly!" Zach sounded disgusted. "He's got his meter thingy!"

"Man! Doesn't he sleep?" Chucky shook his head.

Philip lowered the flap and they stared at each other. "We have to do something about him."

"Yeah," Zach agreed, "but what? He scares me."

Philip sat back against his pillow, still whispering. "We'll have to take turns watching him."

Zach snorted. "We can't watch him day and night. And as you can see, the man doesn't sleep!"

"Zach is right." Chucky sounded defeated.

"Well, I know someone who would help."

Zach and Chucky stared at Philip. "Who?"

Philip smiled. "Casey."

"Casey?" Chucky wiped a hand over his face. "Not Casey. I have to put up with her enough at home."

"I like Casey."

Philip and Chucky both rolled their eyes at Zach.

"Well, whether you like it or not, Philip is right," Zach continued. "We need her. Admit it, Chucky, she's good at creating a scene."

"Yeah, so?. . ."

"He means a diversion," Philip said.

"Yeah, that's it. A diversion."

* * * * *

In the morning the boys tended to their chores, Philip doing rounds, Zach stocking shelves in the store, and Chucky helping his mom in the snack bar. They met at the pool at noon. Chucky pointed at the blue raft floating in the middle of the pool. "I told you we'd find her here."

Casey wore a bright pink bathing suit. She was sprawled on her back on the raft. A pair of yellow sunglasses with star-shaped frames rested on top of her head, in the middle of a tangled mess of hair. Her legs hung down off the side of the raft, making ripples in the water and her arm was flung across her face, shading the sun.

"Are you sure you want to tell her?"

"Chucky!" Philip looked peeved. "We have to. Who else could we possibly tell?"

"We can tell Mr. Nesbitt."

"Sure, Chucky." Zach snorted. "And he'll rush right out to help us keep an eye on that ghost wrecker!"

Chucky fished a yo-yo out of his pocket and let it unravel. It hit the end of the string and traveled back up. "Okay. So we tell her." He paused. "No. I won't. You tell her."

Casey sat up on the raft, rubbing at her eyes. "Oh, hi, guys!" She looked around. "Is Jared here?"

"No. Just us," Philip said.

"We kinda wanted to talk to you," Zach added.

Casey started paddling, bringing the raft toward the edge of the pool. "Me?"

Zach sat down on the edge of the pool, slipping off his sneakers. He sank his feet into the cool water, then, patted the concrete beside him. Philip and Zach sat down also.

"Yes, you," Philip said, pulling off his shoes.

Casey was almost to the edge. "Why did you want to talk to *me*?" She looked skeptical, as though waiting for a punchline in another cruel joke.

"We need your help," Zach said.

"Aw, geez!" Chucky stared at his lap and shook his head. "Do you *have* to make her feel important?"

Philip cleared his throat. "It *is* important. Casey, we need your help in something that is important."

He had her full attention. She was sitting very still, listening, waiting for Philip to continue.

"Can we trust you to help us out without telling anyone else what is going on?"

"Can we trust you not to blab to Mom?"

Zach glared at Chucky. "Can we trust you to be there for us?"

Philip cleared his throat again. ". . . and to be there for Jared?"

Chapter Four

Enlisting Casey

Casey stared at the boys, her face solemn. Then she nodded. "If it's for Jared, I'll do whatever you want."

Philip sat down beside Chucky. "It's for Jared and all his friends," he said, peeling off his sneakers and socks. Then, as he bobbed his feet up and down in the cool blue water he told Casey everything they knew about Skelly and his funny-looking gadgets.

Casey's eyes were wide as she listened. "Do you think he can really do that . . . make ghosts disappear forever?"

Zach snorted. "He says he can. And he looks mean enough to do it without a care."

"But we don't really know." Philip's voice was strong. "We just don't want to take chances."

Chucky sat down on the concrete, his legs crossed Indian style. "He scares me," he told Casey.

"You know, before I met the corporal, I would have been cheering for a guy like Skelly. I mean, who really wants a ghost hanging around? But Jared has changed all that."

Casey, Zach, and Philip nodded.

Chucky shook his head, his voice softening. "And Boo has changed all that," he added.

"So what do you want *me* to do?" Casey looked at the boys.

"Whenever you see Skelly and you know that Jared is around—"

"Or Boo," Chucky interrupted.

"Or Boo," Philip continued, "we need you to help us create a diversion."

"A diversion?"

"You know," Chucky said impatiently. "Get his attention, so he forgets about the readings on his dumb old meter, so he forgets about the ghost."

Casey still looked puzzled.

"Remember that time you told Mom I was going to jump off the high dive, so she would run out and check on me, but you really wanted to get rid of her so you could sneak in my room and steal my best Game Boy game?"

"I wasn't going to steal it! Only borrow!"

"Steal, borrow, it doesn't matter now," Philip said. "What Chucky is trying to show you is how you got your mom's attention away from you and onto something else. You created a diversion. That's what we want you to do with that old Skelly. Get his attention away from Jared and onto something else."

Casey's face lit up. "I can do that! It'll be fun. Just like acting!"

"Good." Philip pulled his legs from the water and stood up, brushing concrete dust from his bottom.

"Does that mean I can hang around with you guys?" Casey looked hopeful.

"No!"

"Yes!"

Casey looked from Chucky to Zach. Then Philip answered. "You'll be spending more time with us than usual."

"Okay." Casey pushed away from the side of the pool, watching Zach stand and grab his shoes. "Where are you guys going now?"

"We're going to lunch, then to check on the garden," Zach said.

Chucky glowered at Zach.

"Okay," Casey said sweetly. "I'll see you at the garden in a little while."

They walked down the gravel road that led from the pool, around the campsites and up to the back of the camp store. Chucky was practically flinging the yo-yo. "I hope you guys are happy," he growled. "Now I'll never be able to shake her!"

* * * * *

Zach was on his knees, pulling weeds in the center of a garden row when he heard someone coming up the path. His belly was full from a late lunch at the snack bar and he didn't really want to use the energy it took to swing around and see who it was. When he finally looked, he hissed, "Skelly!" to Philip and Chucky who were each a row away.

Sure enough, Skelly was lumbering up the path. He was humming, holding the meter thing out in front of him as he walked. As he got closer, Zach recognized an old folk tune. *Why's he so happy?* Zach wondered.

"Act normal," Philip warned. Then he raised his hand to wave.

"Philip!" Zach sounded disgusted.

Philip made a face at Zach. "It'll be easier to lead him away from Jared if he trusts us," Philip rationalized.

Skelly raised his hand in a half wave, then veered toward the garden. "Gentlemen, did you know that you are living in a hotbed of ghosts?"

Chucky's face looked blank. "We are?"

"Yes sir. I was getting readings all night. I think I may have sent a few off and on their way, but I won't be sure until I spend more time here. Why, just last night in this area . . ." He paused. "There could be one close by now," he said, swinging the meter in a wide arc.

Chucky stood up. Boo was coming over the hill, bounding toward him, ears flapping as he ran, tongue hanging out. His edges looked fuzzy, like a fog dog.

"Boo!" It slipped out before he could stop it.

Skelly rolled his eyes. "Very funny, son," he said. "You can say boo and make fun all you want, but my meter doesn't lie." His voice had changed, gotten harder. He stopped talking, spun around, and pointed the meter right at Boo!

"Zach! Chucky! Hello, Philip!" Casey bounced around the corner. The star sunglasses that had graced the top of her head were now in place, making her eyes look big, and she swung her pink flip-flops in one hand. As soon as she saw Skelly with his handheld meter, she froze. Then she saw Boo. In less than a moment she sprang into action.

Casey leaped straight up and a scream that would scare the devil himself pierced the air. "Aaaaggghhhhh! I ste-e-e-pped on a bee."

Skelly jumped, almost dropping his meter. "My dear . . . ," he stammered.

"Oh, no!" Chucky ran to Casey, his face masked with concern. "She's allergic to bees. Mr. Skelly. Help me get her inside."

Skelly slipped the meter into his pocket and moved toward Casey. "Let me see your foot," he commanded. "We need to get the stinger out."

"No! I want my mommy!" Casey clutched her foot, hopping up and down. "Don't touch it. I want my mom-m-my!"

Chucky was impressed. Real tears coursed down Casey's face.

Skelly looked like he didn't know what to do. He moved forward awkwardly, to let Casey lean on him. He led her toward the camp store. Chucky dropped back to check on Boo.

Boo bounded toward him, stopping at Chucky's feet. He stooped and patted the pup's head. "Go on!" he whispered. "Go on and get outta here. It's not safe."

Boo sat still, looking upward, a sad look on his face as everyone followed Casey and Skelly inside the camp store.

* * * * *

Sometime after dinner, Zach and Philip sat down on top of the picnic bench by the snack and soda alcove to wait for Chucky. He was to meet them there. Already the sun was setting and the near dark made it hard to see under the shadowy tree.

"Philip, I think we have Chucky's mom worried," Zach told his brother.

"How's that?"

"I heard her talking to Dad at the registration desk. She said she'd seen Casey talking to herself twice this week. She said she'd never seen her get so hysterical about a bee sting before."

Philip leaned forward and put his elbows on his knees and rested his chin in his open palms. "We'll have to tell Casey to be careful," he said with a sigh. "This whole thing is a big mess. Darn that Skelly."

"Yeah. He sure has stirred up a hornet's nest." Zach smiled, impressed at his own comparison to

Casey's diversion. "Hey, here comes Chucky now, and he's got Casey with him."

Philip looked up. "Well, I'll be. He did bring Casey, and he doesn't even seem to mind."

"That was some good acting, Casey!" Zach couldn't hide the admiration in his voice.

Casey grinned. "It *was* pretty good, wasn't it?"

"Shame they didn't find the stinger."

Casey kicked her brother. "That was mean, Chucky."

Philip sat up straight and stretched his legs out across the picnic bench's seat. "What did your mom say?"

"She said it didn't look like anything stung me." Casey laughed. "But I told her it really hurt and she gave me some ice to put on it."

"I hate to trick your mom like that," Philip said. "But it worked. You got Skelly away from Boo. You did a great job!"

Casey beamed. Then her face sobered as she squinted into the early evening darkness. "Hey, isn't that Skelly now?"

Philip looked. "Yes. He never quits, does he?"

"I wonder how he does it," Casey said. "How does that meter thingy work, and where does he send ghosts too?"

"Hmmm." Zach blew upwards. "I'd like to know that too."

Philip leaped from the picnic bench. "I think I'll ask him."

Zach jumped up too, grabbing Philip's arm. "Don't, Philip. Leave him to his spirits. I don't want to know that bad."

Philip shook Zach's hand from his arm. "Well, I do," he said, stepping off toward Skelly and his gadgets. "Skelly. Wait up there. I've got a few questions for you."

Chapter Five

Skelly's Wake-up Call

Zach and Chucky stood to follow Philip out to meet Mr. Skelly. "I hope he knows what he's doing," Zach said, then turned to see that Casey had decided to stay behind at the picnic table. She wouldn't be alone though. Jared Scott was there at the end of the table, his bluish glow, invisible to everyone but the three boys, tinting Casey's blond hair.

Zach waved a hand at him, and Casey waved back. Zach smiled. Casey didn't know Jared was behind her! Jared winked at Zach, who smiled.

The boys approached Mr. Skelly. "Hello," he greeted them.

"I hope we're not bugging you," Philip said, "but we were interested in those things you use there. I know you said one was a temperature gun, but what do they do?"

Mr. Skelly's eyebrows rode up higher on his forehead. "Sure, I'll tell you about them." He looked around quickly, then waved to the ground. "Let's sit down, and you guys can hold them."

So the boys sat in a small circle with Mr. Skelly. Philip felt a little funny about it, almost like he was betraying Jared, who usually made up the fourth person in their circles.

"Now this was all standard ghost-hunting equipment, until I got tinkering with it. But it is basically the same as when I got it." He handed the first thing to Philip. "This is an electromagnetic field meter, also called an EMF. The digital display window there will give a readout of numbers, and it measures static electricity and magnetic fields. Like, if you held it over a tape recorder using magnetic tape it would register a change."

The EMF meter was passed around the circle. Mr. Skelly had turned it off so Chucky couldn't see how the display would work. "Can you show us how it works later?" he asked. Zach jabbed him in the ribs, and he realized he shouldn't have asked to see it work. They didn't want him to use it at all! But he couldn't help it. He liked gadgets, and he was curious.

"I will," Skelly said, then handed the second gun-like thing to Philip. "This is a thermal scanner, or temperature gun. It reads digitally like the EMF, and it measures the temperature. If there is a drop or rise of more than twenty degrees at a spot, then that's usually a sign that there is an anomaly."

"A-nom-al-ee?" Zach asked. "What's that?"

Mr. Skelly looked up in the sky for an answer. "Mainly it means something that can't be accounted for. For instance, if I were in the kitchen where a big turkey dinner was being cooked, I wouldn't expect the temperature to drop twenty degrees anywhere in there. If it did, I would have to assume it was an anomaly. And like at the campfire last night . . . the scanner picked up a drop of nearly thirty degrees. That's when I point the camera at the spot and shoot."

Philip passed the temperature gun to Zach. "So how did you change these things?"

"Oh, I put audible alerts on them. I put a beep into them, which will only sound if they register a certain amount of change. This way, I can even set the EMF down somewhere, and it will let me know when something is around."

Chucky squirmed. The whistle he had in his back pocket was starting to jab him. "So you find a ghost, take its picture, and then what?"

"Yeah," Philip said. "How do you get rid of ghosts like you said you can?"

"That's hard to describe. I developed the method myself. So far the three houses I've used it in have remained quiet. Like I said before, most people who do this sort of stuff don't agree with me. The group I'm in at home doesn't like me to use my method. I zap ghosts with energy. I believe it repels them, sends them away for good."

"What do you zap them with?"

Mr. Skelly had a curious look on his face. He paused. "It's something of my own making. I got the idea from cattle prods. A cattle prod is a long rod with an electrical charge at the end. You touch a lazy or contrary cow with it and you can get it to go anywhere you want."

Chucky shivered and made a mental note to stay away from Skelly if he was carrying anything that looked like a cattle prod.

"So I made this," Skelly said.

He pulled what looked like a cellular phone from one of his vest pockets. With a click of a button the antenna shot up. He held it out in front of him, parallel with the ground, then he stared at Zach who was at its other end. "Don't worry, it's not on. Now, if I pushed this button it would send out a nine-volt charge, which isn't much, unless you are made of ghost stuff."

Philip clapped his hand over his mouth. *That would never work in a million years!* He noticed Skelly's look. "Does it hurt them?" he asked, trying to look serious.

"It must work. It *has* worked. Of course, it's only my opening shot. I zap them over and over, directing psychic energy at them at the same time. Psychic energy is powerful in itself."

Philip remembered how Mark Nesbitt sometimes wrote of psychics, how they were able to communicate with ghosts, and sometimes were able to lead a spirit to the white light. He wondered if Mr. Skelly truly did have psychic powers. If he did, that could be far more dangerous than his nine-volt shooter.

"Now then," Mr. Skelly said, putting his energy shooter away. "Do you want to go hunt some ghosts? I was on my way to the field where I picked up that orb. I'll let you hold the scanner."

Philip jumped up and did some scanning of his own. He didn't see Jared or Boo anywhere. The change in Skelly's demeanor put him on edge. *He was being too nice.* "That would be okay," Philip answered.

Zach jumped up too. "Do you think we should?"

"Dad won't care," Philip said, hoping Zach would relax. As long as they were with him, he couldn't really find much, could he? Not Jared anyway.

Mr. Skelly handed the scanner to Chucky first. "You go ahead and try it for a while." He showed Chucky how to turn it on and hold it out in front. Chucky watched the numbers flash fast in the display window, then settle down to .77.

"Now, while we walk around, hold it steady. Don't let it point up or down, just straight out. The numbers will change a bit here and there. If you get near a building it will go up because the building is warm. In the woods it will drop some. If it jumps or dives more than twenty degrees the alert will sound and it'll shoot a picture in whatever direction you are pointing."

"Okay," Chucky whispered. He couldn't help being a little excited. "Don't get in front of me, guys," he said.

"That's right," Mr. Skelly said. "A person will warm it up."

They started off in the direction of the field. Zach walked alongside Chucky, watching the scanner reading fluctuate and checking around for any sign of Jared. Philip was beside Mr. Skelly.

Philip watched the reading on the EMF. He didn't really understand what it did even after Mr. Skelly had told them. "What does static electricity have to do with ghosts? Isn't that what makes a sweater throw sparks when it's been in the dryer?"

"Yes, exactly. Do you know how in a lot of ghost stories the people say the hair stood up on the back of their necks or raised up on their arms?"

"Yeah," Philip answered, remembering that it had felt that way when they first saw Jared.

"Static electricity can cause your hair to stand on end. People just started noticing that having a ghost around would do it too. Then, when they put the two together, they came up with the idea of using the EMF for ghost hunting and it's proved itself."

Just then the EMF beeped. Philip looked but didn't see anything. "Hey!" Chucky yelled just as his scanner beeped.

"Here!" Mr. Skelly handed the EMF to Philip and quickly pulled up his digital camera to snap a photo. In the split-second flash of bright white light Philip thought he saw something blue. Everyone crowded close to see if anything was going to show in the photo.

"Rats! Darn bugs," Mr. Skelly said.

The boys couldn't help laughing. There on the photo was a big moth. It was blurry, with its wings beating fast, but it was definitely a moth. Skelly's eyebrows came together and he looked angry. He held his meter up again. "Whatever it was, and it was something besides that danged moth, it's gone now."

The boys looked at each other, relieved. That had been a close call.

* * * * *

The next morning bright and early, after a breakfast of bacon and eggs, Philip and Zach rode their bikes on a round of the campsites. "I wonder how long he stayed out wandering around last night," Zach said. "I wish Dad could do something about it."

"What can he do? You can't put a curfew or anything like that in a campground. Dad wouldn't care if he walked around til dawn looking for ghosts."

"I guess he's in there sleeping now," Zach said as they neared Skelly's site. The pop-up camper was quiet; no smell of breakfast there.

Philip braked his bicycle. "Do you really think he's asleep?"

"Wouldn't you be if you'd been walking around all night?"

"I probably would be," he said, poking his glasses up his nose. "And I'd be really ticked if someone made a lot of noise outside while I was trying to sleep."

Zach's eyes widened. He cupped his hands around his mouth. "Hey, Chucky!" he yelled at the top of his lungs. "We're down here!"

Philip tucked his chin down to his chest and laughed. Most of the other sites looked active, so he didn't worry about waking others. "Do it again," he whispered.

"Chucky! Get a move on!"

Philip grinned and winked. "Bang on that trash can, Zach, so he knows where we are!"

Zach stifled the urge to laugh, then started banging on the big metal trash drum next to Skelly's campsite.

Something moved behind one of Skelly's windows. "Okay, he's up," Philip whispered.

"We're going without you, Chucky!" Zach yelled, knowing their friend was behind a sink full of dishes and couldn't possibly have heard him.

Giggling to themselves, Philip and Zach pedaled their bikes down the lane, waving at the campers who seemed to be wondering what was going on.

Chapter Six

Skelly Zaps a Ghost

"Boys, don't run off. I want to talk to you."

Philip and Zach were just heading to the sink with their supper plates, ready to go meet Chucky by the stables. "What's up, Dad?" Philip asked. He didn't like the serious look on his father's face.

"Come, sit down."

They took the seats they had just left, at the kitchen table. Philip poked the glasses up the bridge of his nose.

"Mr. Skelly was in the store this afternoon. He's a little put out by you two."

"What did we do?" Zach yelped. Philip rolled his eyes. Zach had asked that a little too quickly, and with a guilty tone as well. He could tell Dad had caught it too.

"Oh, something about you two waking him up quite rudely this morning with shouting, and a banging of the trash can. Do you want to tell me what it was about?"

Zach looked at Philip. Philip cleared his throat. "We didn't do it on purpose if we woke him up." He hoped his face didn't look as hot as it felt. He wasn't a good liar; didn't like lying. But he couldn't tell Dad why they'd done it.

"We thought Chucky was following us and we hollered for him," Zach said.

Mr. Baxter took a sip from his coffee mug. "I'm not sure what you did, or why. But Mr. Skelly was very upset with me because of it. I don't like that. I told him you would apologize to him."

"Dad!" they both said. Philip dug a thumbnail into the place mat.

"He said he didn't want an apology. But he said there was something else you could do for him to make it up. I agreed to it after he said I could drop you off and pick you up again."

"What's that?" Zach blew upwards, lifting the bangs from his forehead.

"I'm going to drop you at Little Round Top at seven, and pick you up at Devil's Den at nine."

"What? Why are we going out there?"

"You are going because you are going to tote and carry for him while he does one of his . . . his ghost investigation things."

Philip sat up straight. "Why are you making us do it? You say we're never to go anywhere with someone we don't know."

"Yeah," Zach said. "You wouldn't even let Mr. and Mrs. Carmichael take us to the diner in town for a big sundae. And they were nice! They gave me scrapple sandwiches!"

Mr. Baxter smiled. "You got your sundaes here, and this is a whole different situation."

"But Mr. Skelly is kind of weird," Philip said. He didn't want to be with that crazy ghost hunter out on the battlefield. It would be a betrayal to Jared, helping Skelly find and get rid of ghosts.

"I'm driving you and picking you up. There are tourists all over that area until dark. I'm sure you will be fine."

"Aw man," said Zach. "I want Chucky to go with us then."

"Okay. I'll ask Gloria." Mr. Baxter got up and went to the wall phone. The boys looked at each other with grim expressions. *So that's why Skelly's been so nice*, Philip thought. *He was looking for free help to tote around his equipment.*

* * * * *

"Over here, boys." Mr. Skelly had the trunk of his car open before Mr. Baxter drove away. "There's plenty to carry, and I want the one with the best handwriting to carry my tablet and pencil."

Zach bit his lip. Skelly knew he had it over on them. His voice was bossy and that just didn't sit right with Zach, who was already afraid of the man.

Philip ended up with the tablet. He had to write down everything that the ghost hunter told him to. Chucky was given a tape recorder with a microphone attached by a wire. He was supposed to switch it on or off as directed. Zach was given the shoulder bag. He wasn't told what was in it, and he didn't want to know.

Mr. Baxter had been right. There were plenty of people around, including a group of Boy Scouts in uniform.

"Don't all these people get in your way?" asked Philip.

"Or wonder what the heck you're doing?" asked Zach.

"Yes and yes," Skelly said. "But in order for you to come along I had to come out before dark. Your dad's rules. The park doesn't close until ten, so I might stay longer and get some real work done."

The small group headed up the bank from the parking area to the top of Little Round Top. Even weird Skelly seemed to pause. It was always awesome to stand there and look down the scrubby hill where men fought, bled, and died, and over to the huge boulders that hid sharpshooters.

"That's Devil's Den," Chucky said to no one in particular, his arm stretched out in front of him and pointing to the boulders that rose high above the ground below. "A lot of soldiers were trapped in there and died."

That seemed to snap Skelly out of his quiet moment. "We'll get there soon enough. Let's get organized over there." He led the way to what the boys had always called The Castle. It was, in actuality, the monument of the 44th New York. But it did look like a stone castle with its tower rising high overhead. A person could walk through its arched doorway to its cool interior during a hot summer day.

Two little kids came squealing out from the inside as they approached. Their squeals had echoed inside it.

"I figure we can start here and walk down the hillside, taking readings as we go. We'll end up over there." He took the bag from Zach and unzipped it. "I've got extra batteries and discs for my camera in there. Don't drop the bag." Satisfied, he zipped it back up and handed it to Zach again. Zach, nervous now for some reason, slung the strap over his head to hang it crossways. The only way it would drop would be if he fell with it. He didn't want Skelly angry with him.

They started a slow walk downwards. Chucky waved a bug away from his face. "I read that days after the battle every fence post and tree was black with flies."

"That's interesting," Mr. Skelly said, but he didn't sound like he meant it. In fact, he was smiling. Chucky shivered and decided to stay quiet. He couldn't help thinking about things he'd read though.

"Philip, write down the fact we are beginning our decline of the hill at 7:15 p.m. And that on this hill a headless horseman has been reported."

Philip did as he was asked. He thought he remembered something about the headless horseman in one of Mr. Nesbitt's books.

All the way down the hill Skelly stopped from time to time to take pictures, telling Chucky to turn on the recorder and Philip to write down things. Zach was grateful he just had to watch the bag. They'd go right, scaling the hill sideways, then down a ways, then go left on the hill sideways. It wasn't easy walking, and Philip didn't see how they'd be able to do it after dark anyway. He also didn't know that hunting for ghosts could be so boring. All they'd had to do was plant a garden and they got one! He thought of the day they'd found Jared Scott's I.D. tag and how badly they were scared when he appeared to them. It made him smile now.

They finally neared the bottom and the road. Skelly turned to take a couple of shots up the hill, not really having a target for these. He took several new discs from the zippered bag and put one in the camera. "I've had this camera forever," he said to no one in particular. "I need one that has memory cards. They hold lots of photos on each card."

The boys gave each other puzzled looks. They didn't know how the cameras worked—only that Jared had managed to get his picture taken by one.

Skelly wasted no time crossing the road to Devil's Den. A paved pathway wound itself in and up through the boulders. Along the way he would find a stopping place, or his meter would beep and he'd take pictures and have Chucky tape a while and Philip write a while.

"I haven't heard so many beeps as I have this evening," Skelly said. "And the temperature variations have been really interesting, too."

"Yeah," Philip said, glancing down at the notebook. He was on the top of his third page of figures. It looked like some kind of math problem. *86 degrees at five yards to left, 67 degrees, five to right. Photo, orb.*

Philip hadn't written this much boring stuff ever in his life! But then, when they reached the topmost boulder of Devil's Den and Skelly had walked out toward its edge to look down, his beeper went off, and he yelled, "Philip! Forty-nine degrees!" He shot a picture, then another.

"My word! The size of this! It's an orb! Chucky, tape!"

Philip's heart beat hard at the excitement in Skelly's voice. *What was going on?* He moved forward without thinking and wrote as he went.

He saw the ghost hunter take his energy shooter from his pocket. The man was so excited he'd thrown the meters down at his feet. With one hand he held the camera up and shot photo after photo as zaps sounded from the antenna on the energy shooter he'd invented.

"Chucky! Get over here! Everybody else move back!"

Chucky went forward, microphone outstretched. He was shaking and didn't want to be that close. Zach hung back and grabbed Philip's arm as he joined him. Two tourists came up the pathway just then, and they stopped behind the boys.

"What's going on?" they asked.

Philip and Zach shrugged. Neither one of them wanted to answer that.

"There!" Skelly yelled. "It's gone! I've proved it. I have it all in the camera!" He turned to the boys, grinning. "Come on, look here." The two people followed along and were going to listen in, but Skelly shooed them off with his hand. Philip couldn't help laughing. His laughter stopped though, and turned sour in his mouth when he saw the series of pictures Skelly showed them when he got them in line.

A bright white streak of light mist sliced through the pictures up and down. There were several photos that looked the same. And then, suddenly the streak was faded, except for a starburst of golden light.

"See, that's a shot of the actual zap of energy hitting the ghost!" Skelly said. "And what happened then? Here you go!" His face was lit with wild excitement.

The last photo showed nothing but the evening sky, a pretty blue with small white clouds.

Philip gulped. The ghost was gone. *Where did it go?*

Chapter Seven

Casey Causes Concern

Philip couldn't wait to get home. When Dad pulled into the parking lot at the top of the hill by Devil's Den he practically leaped into the car. Zach slipped into the front seat next to his dad, and Chucky sat next to Philip. No one was talking.

Dad leaned forward, looking in the rearview mirror until Philip looked up and met his gaze. "Was it that bad?" he asked.

"Yes!" they all answered in unison. Philip noticed that Chucky blushed when Mr. Baxter looked his way.

Dad smiled. "Come on, now. It couldn't have been that awful. Did he work you hard?"

Philip shook his head. "No . . . I mean yes." How could he tell his dad that there was something sinister about Skelly? Dad would want an explanation. Then

54

what? Tell him that Skelly is out to get one of your very best friends, a ghost?

Dad looked puzzled.

"He just doesn't know how to have a good time," Zach put in, and Dad sat back. He seemed satisfied with Zach's answer.

Philip stared at his hands in his lap and swallowed the lump in his throat. He had to talk to Jared. True or not, it sure looked like Skelly had zapped that ghost right off the rock on Devil's Den. And if he had . . . Philip closed his eyes and took a deep breath, well, if he had, then this ghost-zapping stuff was no longer a laughing matter.

A nine-volt battery, for Jezebel's sake! But nine-volt battery or not, the fact was that the orb had disappeared, which meant Jared could be in danger. Skelly was one dangerous character! Philip groaned, wishing he could zap the ghost hunter right off the campground.

Jared found them that evening. The three of them sat looking forlorn on the bench behind the camp store. "You look like my momma did the day I told her I'd signed up to fight in the Union army," Jared said. "It can't be that bad."

It was the second time someone had said that to them in less than a day. *But it **can** be that bad*, Philip thought. How could he explain it to Jared?

"Jared!" Zach jumped to his feet as soon as he realized the corporal was standing there. "We gotta talk to you. Ol' Skelly *can* zap ghosts and you gotta make yourself scarce. You better warn the guys. And stay away from Skelly. I'm scared . . ."

"Whoa . . ." Jared's rough, worn hand landed on Zach's shoulder. "Slow down there, son. Take a deep breath."

"But Zach's right," Chucky added, his face earnest. "We saw it with our own eyes. He zapped a ghost on the rock at Devil's Den. He hit it with his zapper. First there was an orb in the picture, and then there was no orb."

Jared looked confused. "Orb? What's that got to do with me?" He turned to Philip for an explanation.

Philip looked somber. "Skelly has all these tools," he told Jared. "I don't know how they work, but they tell him when there is static electricity in the air, and when the temperature is dropping . . . all signs that a ghost is in the area."

Jared nodded. He didn't seem to be surprised.

"When he gets a temperature drop or sees an increase in static activity he takes a picture with his digital camera. When there is a ghost around, it shows up in the picture as a blob of light. Skelly calls that an orb."

"Hold on there." Jared knitted his eyebrows in concentration. "How do you know that seeing an orb really means there is a ghost? It could be anything."

Zach was shaking his head. "No, Jared. The night he took a picture of you we saw your orb. It really works that way."

"Okay, supposing it does. How do you know he can zap them away?"

Philip gulped, remembering. "His temperature gauge dropped to forty-nine degrees and he went wild, snapping picture after picture. We saw the orb, big and clear in the first few shots. Then the next shot had a big streak across it. Skelly told us that was when he zapped it. Then, in the next picture there was nothing. It was gone." Philip stopped. "We think he zapped that ghost away to somewhere far away . . . but where?" he added.

Jared didn't say anything for a long moment. Then he scratched his jaw and said, his voice almost a whisper, "I'm going to have to follow this Skelly and find out what he is up to."

Philip's breath stopped in his throat. "But . . . you can't . . ."

"No!" Chucky and Zach both shouted. But Jared was gone, faded away in the early evening light.

* * * * *

Philip separated a small gold key out of the clump of keys on his key ring, then bent to insert it into the soda machine door. Even though the sun had only been up an hour, the door was already warm to the touch. That's why he always checked the machines in the morning. By afternoon the metal door would be frying. The door swung wide and he leaned down to peer into the machine. After checking the cans in each row he jotted down the numbers in his notebook so he would know what needed to be filled. Across the way he saw Casey. She was walking backward and waving her arms. He straightened up to listen.

"Come on . . . follow me. Attaboy. You want to come to the stable, don't you, boy?"

Philip leaned against the soda machine and watched Casey. He couldn't see the dog, but he knew she must be trying to coax Boo into following her to the stables. He smiled. Casey got on Chucky's nerves, but she wasn't all that bad.

"Come on. Get up! Don't just sit there scratching your ear like you don't hear me!"

It was obvious from Casey's expression that Boo was having none of it. Philip started to laugh, but he stopped. Gloria Coppersmith had come out of the snack bar and was watching Casey.

"Boo! Do you have fleas or something? Quit that scratching and come on. I have to do my barn work and I want you to come with me!" Casey's hands were on her hips as she stared down at a spot on the ground in front of her.

Philip's hands shook as he tried to wave to Casey, to get her attention, so she would see her mom. But she just kept chattering away.

Gloria's brow wrinkled. She looked like she was about to say something, but then, she shook her head and walked back inside.

Philip shoved his glasses up on the bridge of his nose and closed the soda machine door. After last night when Jared had said he was going to follow Skelly, worry about the corporal had been eating him up. Now Casey . . . what must her mom think?

Stuffing his notebook back in his pocket, Philip turned down the path toward his next soda machine. He guessed Boo had finally followed Casey to the barn. Chucky was probably already there, too. Today was his day to help with barn chores. Zach was in the camp store working with Dad. He needed to round them up to talk.

Philip changed tack, heading for the barn. He'd tell Chucky to meet behind the store as soon as he was done with his morning chores.

* * * * *

"We've got problems," Philip said. It was almost lunchtime and the three of them sat on the grassy edge of the garden. He was sorting the bushel basket of vegetables he and Zach had picked waiting for Chucky to arrive. There were tomatoes, cucumbers, and green peppers. The early summer squash had finally run its course.

"Yeah, we know," Zach said shortly. "I wish Jared would stay clear of Skelly."

"Me too." Chucky used a rag to rub dirt off a big tomato before placing it in the tomato basket.

"Not just that," Philip said. "We have another problem."

Zach looked up from the cucumber he was cleaning off.

Chucky stopped rubbing the tomato. "Now what?"

"Your mom saw Casey talking to Boo today. Of course, she couldn't actually *see* Boo, so she probably thinks Casey is going loony."

"She is loony!"

Zach kicked Chucky. "Do you really want your mom worrying about Casey?"

"No." Chucky reached in his pocket and pulled out a bottle opener. Using the pointy end he pried the green blossom from the top of a tomato. "But, I told her to be careful. What else can we do? She is such a ditz!"

"Maybe we should talk to your mom," Philip suggested.

Zach looked surprised. "And tell her what?" he asked.

Philip rubbed his rag on the top of his bony knee. "I don't know," he said. "I was hoping you guys would have an idea."

Zach picked up a basket and said, "I don't know about you, Chucky, but I am fresh out of good ideas. Come on. Let's take these vegetables inside."

Philip and Zach each carried a basket of vegetables into the store.

Inside, the boys stopped. Chucky's mom was sitting on a stool behind the registration desk. It was unusual for her to be in the store at this hour.

"Hey boys, if you don't mind, we need to ask you a few questions," Dad said.

Chapter Eight

A Dog for Casey?

"It's about Casey," Mrs. Coppersmith said. "She's been acting strange. We wondered if you boys had noticed anything?"

Chucky plopped down on a chair near the cash register. "Geez, Mom. Casey's always been weird. I've been telling you that for years, but you never want to listen."

Philip shot Chucky a shame-on-you look.

Dad pulled out a chair for Philip and Zach to share. "Is there anything you guys could tell us? I know you've noticed it too. You were all there when she went through that dramatic scene with the bee sting."

"And, Philip," Chucky's mom added, "I'm sure you saw Casey talking to herself earlier today. I noticed you were watching her too."

Dad walked behind the counter to stand with Chucky's mom. "Something must be bothering her. Has she said anything to you boys?"

Philip and Zach shook their heads.

Chucky's face lit up, then he took on a serious expression. "I think I know what it is, Mom," he said. "Casey always wants to tag along with us, and . . . well, guys just don't want a girl tagging along. Then last week she started saying she had a dog. I knew she didn't really have a dog, so I ignored her. But now I'm thinking . . . maybe she just wants a dog real bad."

Zach lowered his head to hide the grin that was trying to bust out on his face. *Chucky's using this to try to get himself a dog,* he thought.

Philip latched on to the idea. "She does seem lonely," he said. "There just aren't any girls around for her to play with."

"Well, if that's all it is," Dad swept open the registration book, "she's in luck." His finger ran down the pages of the book. "In two weeks we have those campers coming in from that all-girls' school. She'll find lots of new friends."

Gloria didn't look so certain. "That's just it," she said. "The girls she does get to meet and spend time with always leave. It's not like the guys, who always have each other." She hesitated. "Maybe I should think about getting her a dog."

Suddenly Chucky's expression soured. "Wait a minute," he said. "I've always wanted a dog."

Chucky's mom stood up suddenly. "Chucky, don't go making this into an issue. Right now, I'm worried about Casey, and I'm not even sure about this dog thing. If it's going to cause even more problems I better think hard about it before we get any animals."

His eyes wide, Chucky started backtracking. "It's okay, Mom," he said. "Casey probably does need a dog more than me."

Philip looked at Chucky. He knew how hard it must have been for Chucky to say that.

"It's something I have to think about a little more," Gloria said. "I don't want to rush into anything. The campground keeps us all busy enough."

Philip stood up and Zach sprawled across the chair, happy to have it to himself.

Dad closed the registration book and straightened the desk as though he was finished.

"I'll have to talk to Casey," Gloria said. "It's the only way to know what's really bothering her. If she's making up imaginary dogs and talking to them in public . . ." Her voice trailed off behind the boys as they hightailed it out of the camp store.

They found Casey at the pool. She was sitting at the top of the slide, her arms high in the air. "If anyone is out there, look at me now," they heard her exclaim. "I am going to go down the slide on my belly!"

"Oh, boy." Chucky ran a hand over his brow. "She's getting more and more loony. No wonder Mom is worried."

"Look over there," Zach said, laughing. "She does have an audience. She's smarter than you think."

Chucky and Philip looked toward the far side of the pool where Zach was pointing. Corporal Scott was leaning against the chainlink fence, arms crossed, smiling up at Casey as she maneuvered herself onto her belly. As they all watched, she shoved off, zipping down the wet slide like a seal from a rock and into the pool with a big splash.

"Cool!" The words slid from Zach's mouth in a tone that matched the admiration on his face.

"Cool. Sure," Chucky grunted. "Her cool stuff is just giving Mom more to worry about. She's gonna get the corporal busted. She could have just gone down the slide without talking to herself first."

"Actually, she wasn't talking to herself," Philip said. He pushed his glasses up and swung open the gate to the pool area. "She was talking to Jared."

Chucky ignored Philip and marched across the concrete.

Casey had seen them and was swimming toward the side of the pool. "Did you see me?" She swung her wet hair out of her face and grinned, her face glistening in the hot afternoon sun. "I went down the slide on my belly! Is Jared here, 'cause I think he was watching me? I felt a breeze lift my hair when I was getting into the pool, only I don't think it was a breeze. I think . . ."

"Take a breath, Casey! So you went down the slide on your stomach. We all do it."

Casey's expression deflated like a balloon, but she perked up when Zach said, "It looked great though, Case. And Jared *was* watching you!"

"That is true. I saw it, and she looked quite brave."

Chucky's face turned red when he realized the corporal had joined them. "Yeah, I guess it was alright," he said.

Casey was staring up at the space between Chucky and Philip. "Is Jared here now?" she whispered.

"Yes," Chucky whispered back, and everyone laughed except Casey.

"You're getting us all in trouble, Casey," he said. "Even the corporal."

Casey's mouth dropped open.

"Mom saw you talking to Boo this morning, and it isn't the first time she's seen you talking to yourself," he said.

"I was not talking to myself."

"But Mom doesn't know that! And we don't want her to know that! We warned you to be careful."

Casey sank down so her shoulders were in the water. "I'm sorry. I'll be more careful."

Philip cleared his throat. "We kinda told your mom that you were talking to an imaginary dog. It would help if you'd go along with our story."

"An imaginary dog!" Casey's face turned red. "I am not a baby. I do not have imaginary friends anymore!"

Jared chuckled. "She's a feisty little thing."

"Feisty isn't the word for her." Chucky grunted.

Casey spun around. "What's feisty? Who's feisty? If that means I am angry, then yes, I am feisty," she said.

Philip ignored Casey's misunderstanding of the word *feisty.* "Your mom thought if you were imagining a dog, then you must be lonely."

"I am not imagining a dog!" Casey punctuated her words by slapping the water.

"We know, but Mom thinks . . ."

"Chucky, I don't want Mom to think that!" Casey looked as if she was going to cry.

"So now . . ." Philip continued as though he hadn't been interrupted, "your mom is thinking about getting a *real* dog for you."

"But I don't want . . ." Casey stopped in mid-sentence. "A dog? A real dog? Mom is thinking about a real dog?"

Zach smiled and nodded. "Yeah. Isn't it cool?" he said. "All you have to do is stick to the story about having an imaginary dog so she thinks you are desperate for company."

When Philip looked around he noticed that everyone was smiling. Even the corporal.

An imaginary dog, Casey mused. Then she laughed out loud, a rippling laugh that filled the air. "Yes," she said. "I think I *was* talking to my imaginary dog."

Chapter Nine

Baiting the Hunter

When the boys left Casey at the pool, Jared followed them through the fenced entrance. "Meet me this evening, boys, will you? I still have some friends to talk to, but I think there's a way to get this Mr. Skelly out of our hair."

"What do you mean?" Philip asked, excited that someone, even if he wasn't flesh and blood, had a real idea.

"Just meet me tonight," he said, and faded from their view.

Chucky rammed his hands into his pockets. "I hate when somebody leaves me hanging. But boy, it's worse when they can just *POOF* and disappear!"

"I guess he means after dinner," Zach said.

"And in the garden," Philip added.

Chucky forgot his annoyance at being left hanging and grinned. He thought it was wonderful that they not only knew an actual Civil War soldier, but that they knew him so well he could leave some things unsaid. It was like knowing that a certain look from his mom meant: *Please don't make me ask you again.*

"Let's head back to the store," Philip said. "We should double-check the vegetables and see if Dad needs anything."

* * * * *

Zach carried a piece of chocolate cake out to the garden with him to wait for Chucky. "Chucky's mom sure makes good cake," he said.

"Yeah, and when she bakes one for us it never seems to last more than two days. I wonder *why?*"

"Oh, be quiet."

Philip spread a blanket on the ground by the oak tree stump. "It might be good stargazing tonight for real." Watching the stars and looking for satellites were the reasons they usually gave for lying around the garden at night. They were in sight of the store and the back kitchen window of their small house, and Dad would prefer they stay there rather than running around the campground anyway.

The moon was in its last phase, and even when it rose high in the sky it wouldn't be much more than a sliver. A banana moon, Zach used to call it. The smaller the moon was, the brighter the stars were. When there was no moon at all, the Milky Way could be seen striping the sky.

Chucky joined them just as Philip lay down on his back. "If I were Jared, I think I would fly up there to see the stars," Philip said quietly. "I'd go stand on the moon and watch how the earth rises in the moon sky, like the moon does from here. And I'd go further out and see if the earth would look like a Christmas ball, with tinsel on it."

Zach snorted. "Yeah, right. A Christmas ball?"

Philip sat up angrily. "Yes! It would, I know it would."

"Guys, don't yell," Chucky said and sat down between them. "You are always fighting with each other."

Zach turned to Chucky. "Yeah, we're kinda like you and Casey, aren't we?"

"I didn't mean . . . ," Chucky started to say, but a calmer, older voice broke in from over their shoulders.

"Looks like you fellows don't have time to talk to me tonight."

The boys scrambled around to look up at Jared, who glowed soft blue in the darkening evening. "We're just talking," Zach said. "Come on and sit down."

They moved into their usual circle, with Jared making up the fourth link in the chain. Knee to knee they sat. "What did you find out?" Philip and Zach asked together.

"Quite a lot. First of all, you should know that any harm this Skelly can do is minor."

Philip released a sigh. "Are you sure?"

"Yes. That's according to a certain Texas Ranger who had a run-in with Skelly at Devil's Den. One of the fellows here, who wander, talked to him out there at the Den." He broke off with a big smile. "You boys should know that you are quite famous yourselves."

"Us? Famous?" Chucky asked.

"How?" Zach squeaked.

Jared scratched his chin. "The ranger told our fellow about three boys with a man who kept poking him with that contraption. Our fellow explained who you were, and that you were only trying to keep an eye on this Skelly, and also that you were worried sick about what had happened. The ranger said he'd heard that a cavalryman was seen walking and talking with three boys in this area." Jared chuckled. "So you might say, we tell *human* stories while you tell *ghost* ones!"

The boys laughed. "That's cool," Zach said.

"Triple cool," Chucky agreed.

"Yeah," Philip said. "But we have got to do something all the same. If Skelly thinks he is accomplishing something here, he'll be back again and again."

"That's what we figure, too," Jared said. "So we came up with an idea that just might convince him to change his ways. I'll be honest. Some of the guys think Skelly is nothing to worry about and we should just leave him alone. But some of us feel we ought to give him back a little of what he's been giving us."

"And how do we help you make that happen?" Philip asked.

"That's the thing. You have to figure out a way to get Skelly to go up to Ghost Ring Hill. How much longer will he be here?"

Philip knew without thinking too hard, because he had been counting the days. "He's paid for two more nights. It has to be tomorrow night, if not tonight."

"Tonight?" Zach jumped and the last bit of forgotten cake rolled off his lap, plate and fork with it.

"Who knows what tomorrow night might be like?" Philip said. "It could rain. Or he could have plans. We should go get him now."

"But, Dad won't like it."

Philip was ready to make up an excuse, but Jared interrupted his thoughts. "Zach is right to be careful. We could use the time anyway. Just see what you can do about getting him interested for tomorrow night."

"Okay."

After Jared left, the boys looked at each other. Philip was thinking about how they would get Skelly to go to the hill, and what they could say to his father.

Chucky was excited about Ghost Ring Hill. He'd get to see more soldiers again. When he thought about that night they were there to help a young ghost boy find his parents, he remembered how that Confederate officer had saluted him and he got goose bumps, good ones.

Zach was thinking some of the same thoughts. But one thought stood out more than the others. If

Jared and his friends were planning to scare Skelly off, it might be bad. Just what did you have to do to scare a ghost hunter? And if it were going to be that scary, Zach wasn't sure he wanted to see it. Jared was their friend, and his being a ghost didn't bother Zach anymore. But he wasn't sure he could handle others like that.

"No matter what happens," Philip said quietly, "we have to act afraid."

"Scared to death!" Chucky said excitedly.

Zach thought, *Who needs to act?*

Zach began to consider going inside the store, but then Skelly came around the corner. There weren't any meters in his hands, just a soda. He stopped at the edge of the garden.

"Was that your tomato that I made into a sandwich for supper?" he asked.

"Yup," Chucky said.

"It was very good! Are you enjoying the weather?"

Philip stared at Skelly. *He was being too nice. Maybe he wants us to hulk his equipment again,* Philip thought. Still, he got a creepy feeling, standing next to the ghost hunter. "We were going to stargaze," Philip said. "Aren't you hunting for ghosts tonight?"

"I've been over this ground every night. Not much new to find. There's one that keeps avoiding me somehow. I know he's here, but I can't get close to him."

"It's not haunted down here," Chucky said. "Not like on the hill."

"The hill? What hill?" Skelly asked, his face suddenly lit up.

A day too early! Philip stood up. "There is a hill on the grounds. If we didn't have to get inside we'd show it to you. Say! You're here tomorrow night, aren't you?"

"Yes, I am. Will you take me tomorrow night?"

"Sure. Meet us here at dark."

"Just what is supposed to happen on this hill?"

"We can tell you all about it tomorrow, before we go," Chucky said. He stood up too. "I've got to go. See you!"

"See you, Chucky," Philip and Zach said, then they made a show of folding up the blanket.

"Okay then, boys. I'll see you tomorrow night. Good night."

Philip nodded, holding the folded blanket to his chest. Zach picked up his dish and fork, and they parted company with the ghost hunter.

"That was almost too easy," Philip said.

"That's good, right?"

"Sometimes. But sometimes it means trouble."

Chapter Ten

The Ring of Fear

Philip didn't know what awakened him. His eyes looked side to side in the dark bedroom, then to the window. *A blue man,* Philip thought. Then he sat up and grabbed for his glasses.

"Jared?"

"Shhh. I'm sorry I woke you, but I'm glad as well." Jared walked to the side of the bed and lowered himself onto it by Philip's legs. "Don't wake Zach."

"What is it, Jared?" Philip wasn't sure how he felt. Jared hadn't been in their room since the night that they first found the I.D. tag. Only that time he had scared them half crazy!

"I was thinking about Ghost Ring Hill."

Philip sat up straighter and pulled the blanket up around his shoulder. He could feel a chilly air around Jared that he hadn't noticed in a long time. He took special note of the way Jared didn't get in the way of the blanket at all; it just pulled up right through him. "Mr. Skelly is going to meet us at the garden when it gets dark. Then we are taking him up there."

Jared nodded. "That's good. I want to tell you something. We want to frighten Mr. Skelly. You know that, don't you?"

Philip nodded, and looked over at Zach, who sighed in his sleep.

"The thing is, if we have to frighten a grown man who is used to facing down ghosts, then we might have to get pretty darn scary. Do you follow me?"

"I think so."

"Now, Philip, listen. You tell Chucky and Zach that whatever happens up there is nothing they need to worry about. You tell them that it's all play-acting on our parts. Got it?"

Philip could tell Jared was really concerned. He wouldn't have come into the bedroom to wake him otherwise. Philip looked into Jared's blue eyes and made himself smile. "We trust you, Jared. In fact," he whispered, "all you have to do is give us a high sign and we'll get out of there."

"That's my boy," Jared said.

The way he said it made a lump form in Philip's throat. Then, Jared laid one cool hand on Philip's arm and lifted it back up just a bit. In the blue glow Philip could see the hair on his arm try to follow the hand, to stand up on end. "Hey, Jared. That's static electricity."

Jared laughed quietly, then stood and went over to Zach's bed. He reached down to touch Zach's head, and Philip could see Zach's bangs sort of ruffle with a breeze. Jared turned to Philip again.

"Good night, Philip."

"Good night."

Philip didn't get to see Chucky and Zach alone until after lunch when they grabbed their bikes for a midday drive around the campground.

"That was good!" Zach said. "I love fruit salad!"

"You love everything," Philip said.

Chucky was put out and he let them know it. "Did you see Casey? Hiding bits of food in her bag when Mom would look at her. She's really going for 'Actress of the Year' with this imaginary dog thing. She's going to get a dog! Her! It's just not fair!"

Zach jumped on his bike. "If she does get a dog, you get it too, don't you see that? It's going to live at your house! You can win it over to your side."

"Hey! I never thought of that!"

"I need to talk to you about something," Philip said. "I saw Jared last night. He came into the room."

"What?" Now, Zach looked upset.

Philip pedaled slowly onto the wooded campsite lane. He told his brother and friend everything Jared had said during the bedroom visit. Everything, that is, except how Jared had called him "my boy" and how that had made him feel proud and humble at the same time.

"I guess it's going to look pretty scary," Philip said.

"I'm not afraid of them," said Chucky.

"I'm not either," Zach said. *Aw man!* he thought. *This is what I was afraid of!*

Philip nodded. "Good. I told him to give us a high sign so we could get out of there. I think I'll take that sign as a *See you later*, and do just that. You guys can stay if you'd like."

"I'm going with you," Zach said.

"I'll have to decide then," Chucky said. "Have you figured out how and where we will meet him tonight?"

"Tonight there is no moon," Philip said. "I'm going to tell Dad that we are going high up on the hill for stargazing. He knows how I like my stars."

"Don't you feel bad when you tell your dad a lie?" Chucky asked.

"Not if it's for something like this. I want to get rid of Skelly, to get him to rethink his ways when it comes to hunting down innocent ghosts. Jared is going to help us do that, and we have to be there. That's all there is to it. Right, Zach?"

"Hmmm?" Zach's bike wobbled on the lane. "Oh, yeah. Right."

Zach just wanted to get the whole thing over with. He fretted about it that afternoon and could hardly eat his supper. Even Mr. Baxter had wondered if Zach was feeling okay, which made Zach perk up to finish the food on his plate. But he didn't go back for seconds. Then it was evening, and dark before he knew it.

The boys heard Skelly approaching before they saw him. He was whistling that folk tune. They gave each other knowing looks and nods, and Chucky whispered, "Let's do it!"

"Good evening, boys. Are we ready?"

"We sure are. Follow us." Philip flicked on his flashlight and skirted the backyard to head into the field that lay at the bottom of Ghost Ring Hill.

"You were going to tell me a little about the hill, weren't you?"

"Just wait until we get to the bottom," Philip said over his shoulder. He didn't want his father looking out the window in time to see Mr. Skelly joining them on their walk. As far as he knew, they didn't like the man, and seeing them with him would raise alarm bells.

At the bottom of the hill they stopped. "Do you want to gear up?" Philip asked.

"I've brought my camera and energy repeller, but will carry them myself," he said gruffly. "One of you could carry and use the thermal scanner, though." Skelly looked right at Chucky. Chucky held out his hand.

"Sure, Mr. Skelly."

"Okay. So, what is it that makes you think this hill is haunted?"

Philip bit his lip. Skelly looked impatient. *I should have had a story ready*, Philip thought. "Well, some people who went up there one night last summer came back down with a fantastic story," he said. He was a little nervous to find that Chucky and Zach were looking as interested as Skelly. "They saw a ring of ghosts, all different soldiers, and they found they were in the middle of the ring somehow. They said it was terrifying. They also said it felt cold . . . freezing!"

"The soldiers had appeared one by one!" Zach added.

"And they left that way, too," Chucky said. "And one of them saluted."

Skelly snorted and laughed coldly. "I don't think so, I just don't think that's true. I've never heard of anything like that ever happening." He looked hard at Chucky. "You boys better not be pulling my leg," he said.

"We're not," Zach said quickly.

"It did so happen," Chucky said, then caught himself when Philip shook his head at him.

"Mr. Skelly," Zach said. "You probably weren't going to do anything tonight anyway. Come with us and you'll see we aren't telling you stories. Let's see if your equipment can pick up something."

Skelly looked at his watch, then up the hill. "All right. Let's go."

They were quiet during the climb to the top. It wasn't a hard climb, but there were so many small shrubs and tree roots that seemed to come from nowhere, that they had to take their time. Chucky was anxious to get there and see what Corporal Scott and his friends were going to do. And he was anxious to see the soldiers again.

Philip was tense, but eager. He wouldn't let the ghosts scare him. He knew it wasn't meant for them. He would make Jared proud of him.

Zach was trembling. He knew that Jared and his friends wouldn't hurt him, but in a funny way he knew he'd react without thinking that. And funnier yet, he felt sorry for Mr. Skelly who was climbing so nonchalantly up a hill to something that might make his hair turn white. He wondered what Skelly would look like with white hair and a white goatee.

Philip didn't turn his flashlight off until they stood in the clearing. He couldn't help but look up at the sky with its bright stars and he followed the Milky Way as far as he could. Crickets chirped all around, and Philip swatted away a mosquito.

"This the spot?" Skelly asked.

"Yes, sir."

"Chucky, will you scan the temperature?"

Chucky turned the thermal scanner on and swung slowly in a circle, holding the gadget out in front of him. "Seems to be holding steady around seventy-six degrees."

As prepared as Philip thought he was, it all began too quickly. The first thing anyone noticed was the way it went so quiet. Even the crickets stopped chirping. And then Chucky said that the temperature was dropping.

Zach tingled from head to toe and backed himself into the cover of a pine tree at the edge of the clearing. He watched Chucky swirl around with the temperature gun. The numbers were flashing, the temperature going cold fast. He saw Skelly grab his energy zapper. Philip was standing still, but he waved his arm.

"Oh my!" Skelly said, sounding a little concerned. He spun around. "This is wild!"

Zach saw the lights as they came from the trees. A chilling breeze full of white lights swept past him and into the clearing. He bit his tongue so he wouldn't cry out. Philip moved over to Chucky and grabbed him by the arm, pulling him along, and they both joined Zach who was cowering in the boughs of evergreen.

"I want to be there," Chucky hissed.

"No you don't," Philip said, and turned Chucky so he would see what was happening.

Light flew all around Skelly, who was snapping photos and shooting little sparks into the lights from his zapper. "Boys!" he yelled. "Boys, where are you?"

Zach covered his ears so he wouldn't hear Skelly's cries. But he couldn't make his eyes stay shut. It seemed too strange, hearing a hard man like Skelly cry out. He saw the way the circle of light got smaller and tighter around the man who stood in the center, and who threw his arms up over his eyes. Skelly dropped the zapper. The camera hung unused around his neck.

"Boys!" Skelly's breath frosted in the glowing chill air.

Philip put an arm around his brother. "It's all right, Zach. It's Jared. We are okay."

"But, Skelly . . . ," Zach whispered.

"They won't hurt him, you know that."

Just then, they saw Jared appear out of the light. A whistling sound pierced the air. They saw it came from a sword that Jared held high above the ghost hunter's head.

Zach gasped and finally covered his eyes. But Chucky and Philip saw how the lights broke away behind Skelly, and how the man turned and ran screaming down the hill toward the campground.

The boys didn't move. They stayed frozen in their cover until soft laughter came to them from the circle of light.

"Where are my boys?" a voice said, sounding so different from the one who had cried out a moment before.

Zach looked up and saw Jared, not frightening at all. "Here we are!" Zach called and ran toward the corporal. Jared got down on one knee to meet the boys.

"You scared him good!" Chucky said to Jared, then looked around at the men who were forming one by one from the lights. Some faded immediately, but others stayed for a moment or two to nod at the boys or say a word to Jared.

Zach wished Jared could hold him like a real person. As if Jared could read his mind, he looked at Zach. "You were very brave," he said, and smiled. "Now, you ought to go find your Mr. Skelly. And when you do, ask him what happened to him that he left you alone on the hill. Remember, you didn't see a thing."

Zach nodded and took a deep breath. "I don't think he'll want to go looking for ghosts after this."

"It's not likely," Jared agreed. "Say, Chucky. I think someone wanted to have a word with you."

Chucky followed Jared's pointing finger. A Confederate officer wavered in a foggy cloud. Chucky swallowed and walked toward him. "Good evening, sir," he said and saluted the ghost.

"As you were, young man," the officer answered, saluting him back. "I told your friend Corporal Scott I would be honored to lead any action you feel fit to direct. It's been nice seeing you again." With that, he faded into the night.

Chucky felt like he was floating down the hill as they left. Floating, that is, until they came upon Mr. Skelly who lay sprawled on his face halfway down the hill. They shook him gently.

He sat up and grabbed at them. "Where were you? Why did you leave me?" His voice was wild, his eyes darting from side to side.

"Where did *you* go?" Philip said. "You left us up there alone, and we didn't know where you were. Are you okay?"

"Didn't you see it? Didn't you see how they attacked me?"

The boys looked at him calmly. "Who attacked you?"

Skelly sighed and took a deep breath. "Never mind," he said. "Help me up."

Philip shone the flashlight up the hillside path. "We found your zapper up there. I've got it in my pocket."

"Keep it! I just want to get out of here. I want to go home and get back to my job. You can keep the scanner too." Mr. Skelly sounded like a defeated man.

"Gee, thanks, Mr. Skelly." Chucky gripped the thermal scanner tightly. A gadget of his own!

They left Skelly at the bottom of the hill.

"I'll never forget the way he just ran like that," Philip said.

"I'll never forget the way Jared held that sword high above his head and it rang in the air," Zach said.

"It's a saber, Zach," said Philip.

"Saber, sword, who cares?" Zach blew upwards to make his bangs fly.

"Guys! Don't fight," Chucky begged them. "You always fight over stuff like that."

"Aw, listen to you, Mr. Big Shot," Zach said. "Just because you're buddies with a guy with chicken guts on his sleeves . . ."

"It's braid. Officers' braid, Zach," Philip broke in.

"It's called chicken guts too," Zach argued.

"Guys!" Chucky grabbed the energy zapper from Philip and pointed it at them. They froze. "Now that's more like it," he said.

From his hiding place near a large oak tree, Jared watched the boys laughing, their heads together and arms clasped around each others' shoulders. He smiled. *That's my boys,* he thought.

Fact-finders

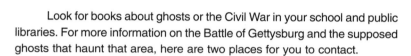

Look for books about ghosts or the Civil War in your school and public libraries. For more information on the Battle of Gettysburg and the supposed ghosts that haunt that area, here are two places for you to contact.

Gettysburg National Military Park
97 Taneytown Road
Gettysburg, Pennsylvania 17325
(717) 334-1124

Or visit the National Park Service on the web at www.nps.gov and follow the links to the park of your choice.

Ghosts of Gettysburg
271 Baltimore Street
Gettysburg, Pennsylvania 17325
(717) 337-0445
www.ghostsofgettysburg.com

Call or write to find out how to order Mark Nesbitt's books or take a ghost tour of Gettysburg. Tell Mr. Nesbitt the Gettysburg Ghost Gang sent you!

If you'd like to see a Gettysburg Ghost Gang Club formed, send a postcard with your name and address to:

Gettysburg Ghost Gang
P.O. Box 70
Arendtsville, Pennsylvania 17303